AF223687

ACKNOWLEDGEMENTS

2020 was a difficult year for many and we were not exempt. We have both experienced the loss of an immediate family member. In spite of our pain, God has been our strength and has allowed us to complete the writing of this prayer journal. His guidance and encouragement as we wrote is why we have been able to press on.

Special thanks to our immediate family members for their unconditional support. Thank you to our editors, designers, and printers for their expertise.

Lastly, we express our love and appreciation to our Kingdom Life Ministries family. Your continual prayers and support, especially during our time of bereavement has been invaluable. We are navigating our way through a pandemic and we will get to the other side of our storms, together. We are grateful for such a special church family.

May God richly bless you all.

DETERMINATION

I Am Pressing On

"I press toward the mark for the prize of the high calling of God in Christ Jesus." **(Philippians 3:14)**

The global pandemic caused by an unseen enemy, the corona virus (covid19), has brought the world to its knees. The lockdown of our global economy has initiated the transition between what the world used to be and what it is becoming. We are confined to our homes, and many are trying to figure out what the future holds. Although we are faced with uncertainty, God is speaking to His people in this season: **"Come, my people, enter thou into thy chambers, and shut thy doors about thee: hide thyself as it were for a little moment, until the indignation be over past"** (Isaiah 26:20).

As Christian believers, we know that there is always hope. The Bible instructs, **"If my people, which are called by my name, shall humble themselves, and pray, and seek my face, and turn from their wicked ways; then will I hear from heaven, and will forgive their sin, and will heal their land"** (2nd Chronicles 7:14). We are God's representatives on earth and He expects the Church to intercede during times of chaos. Some people are worn out by persecution and personal battles, while others are wondering if God is actually hearing them. We cannot afford to lose sight of who we are or who we serve. Let us examine ourselves, confess our sins and keep pressing forward in God.

Our theme is "**The Year of Determination,** *I am Pressing on*". Our determination must be like that of Isaiah, "**...therefore have I set my face like a flint**"; refusing to give up, **determined to win.**

NAME:____

PRAYER PARTNER'S NAME: _______________________________

PERSONAL FOCUS:_______________________________________

FASTING RECOMMENDATIONS

Based on your health, select the most conducive fast that you will be able to maintain for the duration of consecration.

- Biblical fasts were often for one day, from sunrise to sunset. After sundown food would be consumed - Judges 20:26; 1st Samuel 14:24; 2nd Samuel 1:12.
- Biblical fasting involved abstinence from all foods, but not water. Sometimes the fast was not a complete abstinence of food, but a partial fast of a restrictive diet (Daniel Fast - Daniel 10:2-3).
- Our recommendation is that you have one meal per day between 4:00 p.m. and 8:00 p.m. Remain hydrated for the entire day (clear fluids preferably).
- Avoid fried foods, sugar confectionery and carbonated beverages.
- Avoid any distractions that will hinder you from spending quality time with God.
- Limit social media activity to spiritual content.
- Limit television and other recreational activities.

DEVOTION RECOMMENDATION

- Pray for at least 30 consecutive minutes, 3 times each day.
- Read the daily devotional focus, meditate on God's Word and record your thoughts.
- Find a prayer partner that you can connect with for 30 consecutive minutes once a day to pray and discuss the daily focus thoughts.

TABLE OF CONTENTS

AUTHORS' PRAYER

Heavenly Father, we thank you for Your goodness and mercy. Many of us have and are experiencing challenges, but we are grateful that You have kept us alive and in our right minds. We are alive declaring Your wondrous works towards the children of men. We humbly ask for Your divine direction and clear insight as we seek to draw closer to You. Wash us thoroughly with Your cleansing blood, that we may be **"whiter than snow"**. Lord, fill us with Your presence and allow it to saturate our hearts. Help us to have a determined mind. Irrespective of our circumstances, may our consistency in You be unwavering, as we press forward. We are confident that Your love for us supersedes anything we could ever ask or think. With a heart of gratitude, we ask that You undergird us with the strength to press forward and persevere. We declare healing, deliverance, and divine intervention in the lives of Your people. We present the needs of Your people before You, and we believe that all of their needs will be supplied, in the name of Jesus. Lord, we need a refreshing: A renewal of our hearts and minds and a life changing revival in our churches and homes. You are the same God, yesterday, today and forever. You are our only source of help and comfort and we look to You in all things. Thank you for hearing our prayers, in Jesus name. Amen.

DAY ONE

Matthew 14:22-36

TOSSED ON THE SEA OF LIFE

"But the ship was now in the midst of the sea, tossed with waves: for the wind was contrary. And in the fourth watch of the night Jesus went unto them, walking on the sea. And when the disciples saw him walking on the sea, they were troubled, saying, it is a spirit; and they cried out for fear." **(Matthew 14:24-26)**

The church has continued to see itself as a ship amid the changing currents of society. According to Michael A. Turner, the early church came to understand the imagery of the disciples, in a boat tossed by the wind and waves of the sea, to be symbolic of the early church (Pulpit Resource, Logos Productions Inc., 2008). Turner explains that the Latin word for ship, navis is also the root word of the noun, **"nave,"** which is the name for the main part of the interior of a church building from the entry to the chancel. It is where the laity sat to worship.

In light of our current climate, it is as if we are in a boat, being tossed on the sea of life. The times we are living in have brought many of us to a place of frustration and hopelessness. Many of us are struggling against the waves and winds of a society filled with spiritual, physical and economic attacks against our survival. Some of us have come to believe that we are sinking without hope, against the forces of nature. The truth is, as a disciple of Christ, we must emulate our Savior, who has demonstrated that He is above the winds and waves of our world. We must lift up our eyes of faith to Jesus, because He will bring a calm to the storms of life.

Our lesson begins immediately after Jesus had fed the multitude with a few loaves of bread and two small fishes. It was late in the day, and He told His disciples to get into a boat and go to the other side of the Sea of Galilee, while He dismissed the crowd and sought quiet time for prayer. The disciples, many of whom were seasoned fishermen, found themselves in the middle of a treacherous storm. They were tossed about in their small boat by large waves and gusty winds. For hours they rowed against the winds and the swirling sea; becoming cold, wet and exhausted. Panic began to take hold of their emotions, as they continued to struggle against the wind and the waves. During the darkest hour of the night, the fourth watch (3:00 - 6:00 A.M.), Jesus came to them walking on the lake. The disciples were terrified **"It's a ghost,"** they cried out in fear. Jesus immediately said to them: **"Take courage! It is I, don't be afraid."** (Amplified Bible). The storm was battering the disciples, but Jesus saw them and came to their rescue.

Today, many of us are being battered by the storms of life and the waves of adversity. Let us take courage! God is saying, **"I see you"**. He is saying to us:

- I am the door
- I am the resurrection and the life
- I am the way, the truth and the life
- I am the bread of life
- I am the good shepherd
- I am the storm calmer
- I am the one who feeds the multitudes
- I am the one who walks on the waters of chaos

The Bible says that Jesus got into the boat with the disciples and went to the other side. My message is this: Jesus Christ is in the boat with us and He will take us to the other side of whatever we are experiencing. He will take us to the other side of our storms. The simple fact is, that we will get to the other side. This is a great opportunity for the church of Jesus Christ to be the church that God has called us to be, and to live differently than a world that is filled with panic and fear. We are not alone in the battles we are fighting. I encourage you to share your fears and concerns, which is not a sign of weakness, but of trust, faith and confidence in God. Yes, we are being tossed on the sea of life, but we still have Jesus.

MEDITATION QUESTIONS

1. In the storms you are going through, what are your greatest fears?

____

____

____

____

____

2. How is the Church, different from the world, even when we face the same crises?

____

____

____

____

3. What can the people of God do to help our brothers and sisters in this season?

____

____

____

____

PRAYER FOCUS

Pray that God will come to our rescue, step into our boat and take us to the other side of our storms.

Pray for unity among ourselves, as we strengthen and encourage each other.

Pray that God will give us the vision to see His provision; beyond our fears, doubts and insecurities.

Pray that God will bring peace and a calm in the lives of His people.

NOTES

DAY TWO

Exodus 14:1-14

UNDER ATTACK

"And Moses said unto the people, Fear ye not, stand still, and see the salvation of the Lord, which He will shew to you today: for the Egyptians whom ye have seen today, ye shall see them again no more forever. The Lord shall fight for you, and ye shall hold your peace." **(Exodus 14:13-14)**

Jerusalem is a place of prophetic destiny. Of all the cities in the world, none have been so frequently attacked as Jerusalem. As a child of God, from time to time we find ourselves under serious attacks. These attacks are so violent, they leave us sweating, struggling and wondering if we will survive. I strongly believe that the attacks we face are an indication that there is something valuable, powerful and significant in our destiny. The enemy does not want us to get to our destiny and will do to anything to abort God's plan in our lives. These attacks do not come to us because we are lacking in spirituality or because we are outside of the Will of God. The bible demonstrates Jesus as a man walking this earth, frequently under attack, but never lost focus. Jesus continued to operate in the will of His Father and was ultimately victorious over every attack of Satan. It is important that we understand who we are, when we come under attacks and trust God to fight on our behalf.

Exodus 14 depicts a beautiful example of the children of God under attack. The Israelites marched out of Egypt and God provided an angel and a pillar of fire to guide them. When God wanted them to move forward, the pillar of fire or cloud would begin moving. When God wanted them to stay in positon, the pillar would remain still. There was also an angel attached to their camp. The angel and the pillars of fire and cloud, led them to a place where they could march no further. It brought them to the Red Sea by their sides were walls of water and at the rear was their deadly foe, in rage and pursuit of them. It was a time when all hope seemed lost. For many years, the Egyptians kept the Israelites under severe bondage and slavery in Egypt. God heard their cry and sent Moses to deliver them. They escaped Egypt, but remained bound by the wrath of Pharaoh and his men. Before they arrived to the other side of Egypt, fresh terrors surrounded them. Our God who specializes in the impossible, made a way of escape. In Exodus 14:21-22, the Bible states **"And Moses stretched out his hand over the sea; and the Lord caused the sea to go back by a strong east wind all that night, and made the sea dry land, and the waters were divided. And the children of Israel went into the midst of the sea upon the dry ground."**

As a child of God, we may find ourselves in a situation similar to the children of Israel in Exodus 14. What do you do when you are under attack? I pose this question with the answer found in scripture. We are reminded in Psalm 46:10 to **"Be still, and know that I am God; I will be exalted among the heathen, I will be exalted in the earth."** It is important that we do not panic or fear in times of distress. The enemy often uses fear as a warfare tactic against us, but **"God hath not given us the spirit of fear; but of power, and of love, and of a sound mind"** (2ⁿᵈ Timothy 1:7). Let us remember that we are never alone; God is our present help and has promised to fight for us. Although we cannot see Him, or hear Him, rest assured that He is at the forefront of our battles.

In Psalm 121:1 the Bible says, **"I will lift up mine eyes unto the hills, from whence cometh my help."** We will never be defeated as long as we claim victory. If we claim defeat in our minds, we have lost the battle before it has begun. Isaiah 26:3 reads thus, **"Thou wilt keep him in perfect peace, whose mind is stayed on thee: because he trusteth in thee."** I encourage you to commit this scripture to memory, and speak victory as you apply it to your situation.

MEDITATION QUESTIONS

1. Do you believe that the Church and God's people are under attack? If so, how?

____

____

____

____

____

2. How do our struggles impact our destiny?

____

____

____

____

____

3. The enemy often utilizes the weapon of fear against the people of God, how do we counter attack against fear?

____

____

____

____

____

PRAYER FOCUS

Pray that the spirit of fear will not overtake the people of God, but that the spirit of power, love and a sound mind will prevail.

Pray for a focused mind on God as we face the attacks of the enemy, that we will lift up our eyes to the hills.

Pray that God will equip us with the right weapons to fight against the enemies of our soul.

Pray for a continual renewal of strength and confidence.

NOTES

DAY THREE

2ⁿᵈ Chronicles 20:1-29

THE BATTLE IS THE LORD'S

"And he said, hearken ye, all Judah, and ye inhabitants of Jerusalem, and thou king Jehoshaphat, thus saith the LORD unto you, be not afraid nor dismayed by reason of this great multitude; for the battle is not yours, but God's." (2ⁿᵈ **Chronicles 20:15**)

In this life, we will face many battles and struggles. Often times, it puts us in a place of fear and in a place where we do not logically understand why we have to go through that particular battle; why we have to go through that particular struggle or mishap; why us and not someone else? Nevertheless, we must come to a place in our minds, where we make a decision as to how we are going to respond to our battles.

In our text, King Jehoshaphat and the Kingdom of Judah found themselves surrounded by three invading armies. The odds were stacked up against them which brought about great fear. His response was to order Judah to begin fasting as they collectively cried out to God for guidance and help. There may come a time in our lives where we are faced with a predicament, with no option or solution, but to call upon the name of the Lord and to cry unto God in supplication for help. When we get to that place in our lives, it is here that we position ourselves for God to work and for His Glory to be revealed in our lives.

From our text, we see that Jehoshaphat's first response was to lean on God in his time of need. Sometimes we seek God as a last resort, when He ought to be our starting point. He should be the one that we run to when we are faced with a battle. Jesus is the solution to all of life's situations, the remedy to all of our problems, and the antidote that heals all diseases. Jehoshaphat prayed to God with confidence knowing that He was able to deliver. This confidence came through his knowledge and experiences of previous battles that God brought the children of Israel through. When we are going through a battle it is important that we take the time to reflect on

"

the previous battles that the Lord has brought us through. Remembering our past victories will reinforce our faith in God's ability to bring us victory again. In verses 15-17 of the text, we see Jahaziel standing in the midst of the congregation. He had a word from the Lord encouraging the people of Judah not to be afraid because the battle is not theirs, it is the Lord's. Waiting on God is no easy feat, but it is necessary. It is through the waiting process that we surrender to God to work things out for us, and in turn, He will get the Glory out of that situation. As a result of Israel's obedience, the Lord caused the armies of Ammon, Moab, and Mount Seir to begin fighting amongst themselves. When the army of Judah arrived at the lookout point in the wilderness, all they saw were dead bodies lying on the ground.

The Word of the Lord affirms that the battles we face as children of God are not ours to bare – they belong to the Lord. We must accept that we cannot fight battles on our own, and with that knowledge, put our faith and confidence in God to deliver us. It is thorough obedience that we are able to claim complete victory.

MEDITATION QUESTIONS

1. What battles are you facing right now?

____

____

____

____

2. Waiting on God to fight our battles can be difficult. Why is it important to allow God to fight our battles?

____

____

____

____

3. Reflecting on past victories that the Lord has given us is a great reference point to remind us that He can do it again. What are some past examples of victories that God has allowed you to experience?

____

____

____

____

PRAYER FOCUS

Pray that God will allow us not to fear even when the
odds are stacked up against us.

Pray that God will teach us how to wait upon
Him through fasting and prayer.

Pray that God will allow us to have a positive turnaround in
any situation that we may find ourselves in.

NOTES

____

____

____

____

____

____

____

____

____

____

DAY FOUR

Galatians 6:1-10

DON'T GET WEARY

"And let us not be weary in well doing: for in due season we shall reap, if we faint not." **(Galatians 6:9)**

It is important that we know that God will make a way for us, even when it seems like there is no way out. In this scripture, Paul is reminding the Galatians not to get weary in well doing, that in due season they will reap if they do not give up. We can be confident in this same reminder because God is faithful to deliver those who maintain consistency in their service for Christ.

When facing obstacles, the easiest option is to seemingly give up, rather than having a determined mind to press forward. Paul in this text, is challenging us to keep on doing good and to trust God for results. Sometimes we are doing everything that God wants us to do, but we do not see the expected outcome. It is during these times, that we need to look beyond what our natural eyes can see and do what 2nd Corinthians 4:18 states **"…look not at the things which are seen, but at the things which are not seen: for the things which are seen are temporal; but the things which are not seen are eternal"**.

In verses 8-9, Paul encourages the Galatians to sow into the spirit and to continue to do good. Going through affliction, disappointments, injustice, persecution, suffering, loneliness and warfare are all included in the preparation process of where God is taking us. If we want to be all that God has called us to be, we must go through the process. We may get tired because the process is lengthy, but there are no shortcuts or escape routes. As Paul encouraged the Galatians, I also implore you **"do not get weary"**. In this season, I believe that God is taking the church through a preparatory process, to position us in a place where He can use us. We cannot expect to reap the harvest God has promised us, if we do not make up our mind to go through the process. Being willing to go through the process, no matter how long it takes, requires us to have a spirit of determination and perseverance. Even though we may feel exhausted, we need to have an unwavering motivation in our spirit to continue to press forward. Paul told the Church in Philippians 3:14, **"I press toward the mark for the prize of the high calling of God in Christ Jesus"**.

Our focus scripture encourages us to look beyond the present process, and towards the prize we shall receive if we continue to persevere. It is not the time to get weary or give up; but to trust God holistically. With everything surrounding us and the great fear that is upon the nation, the children of God must now, **"be steadfast, unmoveable, always abounding in the work of the Lord, knowing that your labour is not in vain in the Lord"** (1st Corinthians 15:58).

Christian believers be patient and do not lose heart. It is easy to get frustrated, which leads to weariness, but our eternal rewards are far better than any temporal, earthly rewards. There will be times when you feel like you are carrying more than your fair share of the load. There will be times when you are mistreated, but do not become weary in your genuine giving – your labor of love will not be in vain.

MEDITATION QUESTIONS

---

1. What does weariness for the child of God look like?

____

____

____

____

2. What does it mean for us as believers not to get weary?

____

____

____

____

3. What can we do to avoid becoming weary and giving up?

____

____

____

____

PRAYER FOCUS

Pray that the thoughts that make it hard for us to trust God will be destroyed in Jesus name.against us.

Pray that God will give us the strength to keep on going even when we do not feel motivated.

Pray that God will strengthen us so that the cares of this life will not overwhelm us.

NOTES

____

____

____

____

____

____

____

____

____

____

DAY FIVE

Isaiah 55:1-13

TRUST GOD'S TIMING

"For my thoughts are not your thoughts, neither are your ways my ways, saith the Lord. For as the heavens are higher than the earth, so are my ways higher than your ways, and my thoughts than your thoughts." **(Isaiah 55:8-9)**

Timing is important with God. The real test of our faith in God is based on our ability to trust His timing. Trusting God's timing can be challenging, but it is also rewarding once we have mastered the principles of waiting on Him to see us through to the end. I believe that a crucial test of Christian maturity, tests a believer's ability to trust God's timing. Our character and spiritual maturity is developed during the waiting period. Trusting God while waiting positions us for God's Will to be accomplished in our lives.

The principles of trusting God's timing includes waiting on Him through prayer, trusting Him through the process, and remembering His past provisions as we continue to walk in faith. In Lamentations 3:25, Jeremiah reminds us that, **"The LORD is good unto them that wait for him"**. Waiting on God puts us in a position to "birth" a miracle at His appointed time. Waiting on God puts us in a position, where we can see God do something supernatural in our lives.

While in the waiting period, prayer is a key element of the process. Psalms 145:18 says, **"the LORD [is] nigh unto all them that call upon him, to all that call upon him in truth."** Communicating with God through prayer helps us to remain in a close relationship with Him. A consistent prayer life shows God that we are placing everything in His hands, trusting the path He has set us on, and trusting Him to see us through. If we want to please God, we must have faith; because God is the rewarder of those that diligently seek Him (Hebrews 11:6). When your faith is put to the test, it is important to remember the former days that the Lord brought you through (Hebrews 10:32). Our reflection of God's previous provisions, works to reinforce our faith, in knowing that if He has done it before, He can do it again.

Psalms 31:15 says, **"My times are in thy hand…"**, which reminds us that the events in our lives are under God's sovereign control. No danger can happen to us outside of the will of God. **"My times are in thy hand…"** means that everything that concerns us is in the hands of Almighty God. **"My times"**, which refers to my ups and downs, my health and my sickness, my poverty and my wealth; everything is under the control and at the disposal of God. We do not need to puzzle our brains to understand His providence. The hand of the Lord works all things for the good of His children.

Are you willing to let go of your fears and trust God's timing?

MEDITATION QUESTIONS

1. How do you explain Psalms 31:15, **"My times are in thy hand..."**?

____

____

____

____

2. How do we trust God's timing?

____

____

____

____

3. How can we take advantage of a new beginning that God has given to us?

____

____

____

____

PRAYER FOCUS

Pray that God will anoint us to keep our eyes fixed on His
promises while in the process.

Pray that our faith in God will not be shaken in the midst of
temporary circumstances.

Pray that God will remind us of His perfect track record
of kept promises and battles won.

NOTES

____

____

____

____

____

____

____

____

____

____

DAY SIX

Joel 2:1-17

SIGNS OF THE TIME

"For my thoughts are not your thoughts, neither are your ways my ways, saith the Lord. For as the heavens are higher than the earth, so are my ways higher than your ways, and my thoughts than your thoughts." **(Isaiah 55:8-9)**

In our daily walk with God, it is important for us to understand the signs of the time that we are living in. Being able to recognize the signs of the time comes through a deep connection and relationship with Christ. It is through our sincere relationship with Him, that He will reveal to us the signs of the time. When we understand the signs of the time we will know how to operate in time and we will not miss out on what God is doing.

Joel is one of the Minor Prophets in the Bible who had a relationship with God. The reason why he is considered a minor prophet is because of the length of this book, but it does not diminish his role as an available vessel and mouthpiece, declaring the prophetic Word of God to His people. In our text, the Lord spoke through Joel with a central prophetic message to Israel that **"the day of the Lord is at hand"** (Joel 2:1). Joel describes that day as **"a day of darkness and gloom, a day of clouds and blackness. Like dawn spreading across the mountains a large and mighty army comes, such as never was in ancient times nor ever will be in ages to come"** (Joel 2:2 NIV). It was during this particular period that Joel recognized the signs of the time. With an understanding of the times, he sounded an **"alarm"** to let Israel know that they needed to repent and return to the Lord, because the **"day of the Lord"** is at hand.

I believe some of us may have become distracted by the cares of this life. You may have become spiritually stagnant and have missed the signs of the time. In this season, the spirit of God is issuing a **"wake-up"** call to all believers. We must become aware of the fast approaching **"day of the Lord"**; and prepare ourselves to welcome His return.

In our natural lives, an alarm clock is used to awaken us from sleep, so that we can get ready to go to work. If we are too comfortable in bed, we will ignore the sound of the alarm and go back to sleep. We will wake up much later in a panic, having overslept and missed important business. As it is in the natural, it parallels to the spiritual. It is possible to become complacent, even when the signs of the time are calling us to a place of readiness. If we ignore these signs, we may miss what God has for us.

In the familiar Bible story of Noah and the Ark, Noah warned the people that there was a flood coming to wipe out the earth, but they ignored him. As a result, they were wiped off the face of the earth, leaving only Noah and his family alive. Noah preached approximately one hundred and twenty years, and the people ignored his warnings. It is easy to ignore the warnings when we are not seeing visible signs. However, today we are seeing the signs of the warnings issued by the prophets of old. It is time for us to observe the fulfillment of the Scriptures and prepare ourselves, for the day of the Lord is nigh.

MEDITATION QUESTIONS

29

1. What does the topic **"signs of the time"** mean to you?

____

____

____

____

2. How does **"signs of the time"** apply to our day to day lives?

____

____

____

____

3. What strategies can we utilize to ensure we do not miss the signs of the time?

____

____

____

____

PRAYER FOCUS

Pray that God will help us not to miss the signs of the time.

Pray for a renewed reverence for God's power.

Pray that God will give us the courage to trust what
He has revealed to us.

NOTES

DAY SEVEN

Daniel 6:10-22

IN THE LION'S DEN

"Then the king arose very early in the morning, and went in haste unto the den of lions. And when he came to the den, he cried with a lamentable voice unto Daniel: and the king spake and said to Daniel, O Daniel, servant of the living God, is thy God, whom thou servest continually, able to deliver thee from the lions?" **(Daniel 6:19-20)**

In our daily walk with God, it is important for us to understand the signs of the time that we are living in. Being able to recognize the signs of the time comes through a deep connection and relationship with Christ. It is through our sincere relationship with Him, that He will reveal to us the signs of the time. When we understand the signs of the time we will know how to operate in time and we will not miss out on what God is doing.

Joel is one of the Minor Prophets in the Bible who had a relationship with God. The reason why he is considered a minor prophet is because of the length of this book, but it does not diminish his role as an available vessel and mouthpiece, declaring the prophetic Word of God to His people. In our text, the Lord spoke through Joel with a central prophetic message to Israel that **"the day of the Lord is at hand"** (Joel 2:1). Joel describes that day as **"a day of darkness and gloom, a day of clouds and blackness. Like dawn spreading across the mountains a large and mighty army comes, such as never was in ancient times nor ever will be in ages to come"** (Joel 2:2 NIV). It was during this particular period that Joel recognized the signs of the time. With an understanding of the times, he sounded an **"alarm"** to let Israel know that they needed to repent and return to the Lord, because the **"day of the Lord"** is at hand.

I believe some of us may have become distracted by the cares of this life. You may have become spiritually stagnant and have missed the signs of the time. In this season, the spirit of God is issuing a **"wake-up"** call to all believers. We must become aware of the fast approaching **"day of the Lord"**; and prepare ourselves to welcome His return.

In our natural lives, an alarm clock is used to awaken us from sleep, so that we can get ready to go to work. If we are too comfortable in bed, we will ignore the sound of the alarm and go back to sleep. We will wake up much later in a panic, having overslept and missed important business. As it is in the natural, it parallels to the spiritual. It is possible to become complacent, even when the signs of the time are calling us to a place of readiness. If we ignore these signs, we may miss what God has for us.

In the familiar Bible story of Noah and the Ark, Noah warned the people that there was a flood coming to wipe out the earth, but they ignored him. As a result, they were wiped off the face of the earth, leaving only Noah and his family alive. Noah preached approximately one hundred and twenty years, and the people ignored his warnings. It is easy to ignore the warnings when we are not seeing visible signs. However, today we are seeing the signs of the warnings issued by the prophets of old. It is time for us to observe the fulfillment of the Scriptures and prepare ourselves, for the day of the Lord is nigh.

MEDITATION QUESTIONS

1. The Bible says in 1ˢᵗ Peter 5:8, **"Satan goes about as a roaring lion"**. What does this mean?

____

____

____

____

____

2. How do you maintain an effective prayer life?

____

____

____

____

____

3. Do you believe prosperity follows victory after trials? If so, what are a few biblical examples?the time?

____

____

____

____

____

PRAYER FOCUS

Pray that God will allow the spirit of prayer to overtake the body of Christ, as we **"pray without ceasing"**.

Pray for a spirit of consistency in prayer, worship and the Word of God.

Pray against the spirit of jealousy and strife among the people of God.

Pray for victory in lions' den experience.

NOTES

____

____

____

____

____

____

____

____

____

____

DAY EIGHT
Colossians 1:21-29
DON'T LOSE YOUR WAY

"If ye continue in the faith grounded and settled, and be not moved away from the hope of the gospel, which ye have heard, and which was preached to every creature which is under heaven; whereof I Paul am made a minister;" **(Colossians 1:23)**

Intentional planning is a key component in achieving success. Without a clear vision, it is easy to become distracted and lose sight of God's instructions. In spite of what may be happening to us and around us, it is imperative that we strive to stay focused.

Paul was a great apostle and leader, commissioned by God, to spread the gospel all over the world. Paul fulfilled his commission with great diligence and fervor. At the time of our text, Paul was in prison when he heard about the state of the Colossian church. He was informed that there were false teachers promoting errors about Jesus. This infiltration of false teachings led many of the Colossian brethren to deny the humanity and deity of Christ. This teaching sought to obscure the reputation and work of Jesus Christ. Upon hearing this, Paul wrote this letter to the Colossians, because he was concerned that they were losing their way. His aim was to redirect the Colossian brethren back to their faith and confidence in Christ and to expose the heresy and false teaching.

Sometimes, we can get so caught up with the issues of life, that we lose our focus and ultimately end up losing our way. In other instances, we may be focused on trying to figure things out on our own: so much so, that we end up losing focus on the ONE, who is able to navigate us through all of life's ups and downs.

If we lose our focus on God, we will end up missing out on the direction He wants us to go in. If we are not rooted in God and in His word we can easily find ourselves in a place, where our vision is obscured, like the Colossian church. With an obscured vision, we will end up heading in the wrong direction and losing our way to God's desired future for us.

I encourage us all to keep our eyes fixed on Jesus. If we feel like we are getting distracted, go to Him in prayer and He will navigate us through life, regardless of how rough the sea of life may be. God is the **"road map"** of all Christians, guiding us and giving us direction. He is also our compass, keeping us on course. Last but not least, He is our landmark, reminding us of where our focus should be. Let us stay connected to God, look to the Word of God for direction, and give Him first place in our lives.

MEDITATION QUESTIONS

37

1. List three examples of things that can cause you to lose your way.

____

____

____

____

____

2. What can we do to stay on track?

____

____

____

____

____

3. What is the importance of staying on track?

____

____

____

____

____

PRAYER FOCUS

Pray for Divine direction.

Pray that God will reveal our next steps with clarity to
eliminate doubt.

Pray that God will remove the roadblocks in your life.

NOTES

DAY NINE

Luke 13:10-17

THOU ART LOOSED

"And, behold, there was a woman which had a spirit of infirmity eighteen years, and was bowed together, and could in no wise lift up herself. And when Jesus saw her, he called her to him, and said unto her, Woman, thou art loosed from thine infirmity. And He laid his hands on her: and immediately she was made straight, and glorified God." **(Luke 13:12-13)**

The Merriam-Webster dictionary defines loosed as the **"freedom from a state of confinement, restraint, or obligation"**. This suggests that to be loosed means that we were once bound, but are now free. On this Christian path, we face many hardships, that leave us feeling restricted and bound; financially, emotionally, physically, spiritually and mentally. Anyone that has been bound will find that they are at a place of limitation, which leads to feelings of restriction and powerlessness.

When you are bound, you may find yourself in a state of depression. It is one of the darkest moments a person can experience in their life. Feelings of helplessness and loneliness cloud your mind, while desiring to be free. A depressed individual can be surrounded by people, yet feel all alone. It is the will of God that we be loosed and set free from all that confines or restrains us. Freedom from bondage allows us to give God the praise, worship and honor that is due to Him.

In our text, this woman is bent and bound by the spirit of an infirmity for eighteen years. Some of us can relate to being **"bent and bound"**, physically, emotionally or financially. This can come as a result of demonic infiltration or even past failures or disappointments. Be encouraged, it only takes a word from God, for liberation and freedom to come to one that is bound. John 8:36 states, **"If the Son therefore shall make you free, ye shall be free indeed"**. The Bible tells us that Jesus saw the infirmity of this woman and spoke a word of deliverance; **"thou art loosed"**. Immediately after Jesus spoke these words, the woman was delivered from her infirmity.

"Thou art loosed" is a very powerful declaration that we can all subscribe to, given to us from the Word of God. Whether we are going through an illness the doctors cannot diagnose or a **"disaster"** is shattering our stability, today we can declare, **"I am loosed"**. We can be free from the devices of the adversary. No matter what the problem is, God can solve it. Even if everything in our lives seems to be falling apart, God can turn our circumstances around. I declare that thou are loosed, in the name of Jesus Christ.

Take note from our Scripture, that this woman with the spirit of infirmity participated in her deliverance. Luke 13:12 says that Jesus called for her to come to Him. Out of obedience and her willingness to follow His instructions, she received the word of healing and a touch from Jesus that brought about complete healing and deliverance. Like this woman, we also have a role to play in our deliverance. Our role is to trust, obey and remain faithful to God. In doing so, we shall be loosed from whatever is plaguing our lives. Continue to press forward in the Lord, knowing that God's desire is that we are free to worship Him in spirit and in truth. If we are obedient, our lives will be blessed and God will be glorified in us.

MEDITATION QUESTIONS

1. What do you believe that God wants you to be loosed from?

____

____

____

____

____

2. List three examples of hindrances that can block someone from being loosed?

____

____

____

____

____

3. What is the importance of being obedient to God's instructions?

____

____

____

____

____

PRAYER FOCUS

Pray for obedience to God's instructions.

❖

Pray that God will free us from all infirmities.

❖

Pray that God will give us a breakthrough.

NOTES

____

____

____

____

____

____

____

____

____

____

DAY TEN

Mark 4:35-41

JESUS AT THE CENTER OF ALL

"And there arose a great storm of wind, and the waves beat into the ship, so that it was now full. And he was in the hinder part of the ship, asleep on a pillow: and they awake him, and say unto him, Master, carest thou not that we perish? And he arose, and rebuked the wind, and said unto the sea, Peace, be still. And the wind ceased, and there was a great calm." **(Mark 4:37-39)**

Our focus text is a reminder that Jesus is at the center of everything in our lives. The disciples went on a ship with Jesus to get to the other side of the Sea of Galilee. In this instance, we see that the disciples were obedient to the instructions of Jesus while they were on the ship. Even though they were following the instructions of Jesus, they found themselves in trouble. The Bible informs us that **"there arose a great storm of wind and the waves beat into the ship so that is was now full"**. The disciples were expert fishermen who knew how to navigate through stormy situations while at sea. We can assume that they were doing everything in their power to keep the ship afloat and navigate it through the storm. Despite their desperate attempts, they could not control the ship; and with their lives in jeopardy, became afraid.

At times, we will find ourselves in stormy situations. Some of us will make every effort to navigate through our storms, but we may find some of our storms unmanageable. It is in those times, that we find ourselves trapped in fear, even to the point of desperation. The disciples of Jesus went to the lower part of the ship, where Jesus was sleeping. They woke him up, saying, **"...Master thou carest not that we perish"**. Out of fear, they began to question God's care for them. It is a natural response to question how much God cares for us when we are under pressure by the storms of life. It can become frustrating, attempting to understand why God allows us to endure difficulties, while in His company. Jesus got up, rebuked the winds and said to the sea, **"peace be still"**. Jesus turned to the disciples and said to them, **"why are ye so fearful? how is it that ye have no faith?**

To have Jesus at the center, means that He is included in every area of our lives and in every decision that we make. Those of us who have Jesus as our center, have a positive outlook on life and know where to turn in times of trouble. We know that we do not have to die in crisis, because we have God. If we call Him, He will come to our rescue. It is critical that we maintain our relationship with God in consistent prayer. It is important for each of us to have our own personal connection with God. We may find ourselves in situations, having no human help or assistance available to us. When we have Christ at the center of all, we know that we are safe. To have Jesus at the center means that He is living within us and directing us. He will always come to our rescue whenever we call upon Him. He brings life changing transformation and deliverance. When Jesus is at the center, doors that were closed will be opened to us.

When the toils of life seem unbearable, it can be easier to focus on our problems, instead of Jesus, our problem solver. God wants us to get to a place of spiritual awareness, where we know that He will always be there for us. The storms of life are not designed to destroy us, but to increase our faith and give us a deeper experience with God.

MEDITATION QUESTIONS

45

1. What does it mean for Jesus to be the center of our life?

____

____

____

____

____

2. Do you believe we have lost sight of Jesus being the center of everything in our lives? If so, how do we regain this vision?

____

____

____

____

____

3. How can we keep Jesus at the center of our lives?

____

____

____

____

____

PRAYER FOCUS

Pray that God remains at the center of our lives.

Pray that your support system will help to keep you
grounded in faith.

Pray that our prayer lives and our communication with
God will be strengthened.

NOTES

____

____

____

____

____

____

____

____

____

____

____

DAY ELEVEN

1 Peter 2:9-10

CHOSEN FOR THIS HOUR

"But ye are a chosen generation, a royal priesthood, a holy nation, a peculiar people; that ye should shew forth the praises of him who hath called you out of darkness into his marvellous light;" **(1ˢᵗ Peter 2:9)**

According to the Merriam Webster Dictionary, the word chosen means to be selected or marked for favour or special privilege. **"This hour"**, should not be taken literally as a single time frame of sixty minutes. Metaphorically, "this hour" suggests a period or season of time. With this understanding, we can live with the confidence that we have been chosen for this season. In our text, Paul reminds us that we are **"a chosen generation…called out of darkness into His marvelous light"**. As His ambassadors, we have been chosen, selected, called, and set apart with a specific purpose – that we may **"shew forth the praises of Him who hath called you out of darkness into his marvellous light"**. We must never limit ourselves or underestimate how valuable we are as children of God. Once we have experienced the light of Christ, we must endeavour to live a life that reflects His light in a world filled with darkness.

When God chooses an individual, He does not seek those that are qualified, He qualifies those He chooses. To be chosen by God is a high privilege that must never be taken for granted. We are carriers of divine destiny, with purpose and greatness within us. People who come to realize that they are chosen, demonstrate courage and confidence in their daily life. This comes with the realization that, **"it is in Him that we live, move, and have our being"** (Acts 17:28). When God chooses us, no one can stop us from achieving our destiny. In this season, I believe God is calling us to arise and go forward with a spirit of determination. We must seek to press forward with purpose and fortitude, because we have been chosen by God for this hour. Being chosen by God, does not make us superior to others, rather it is a call to service. The call of God comes with great responsibilities and specific assignments. Now is our time to respond to the call of God and to follow Him daily with great faith. As we follow the call of God and walk with Him, He, will take us from where we are, to where He desires us to be. In the process, God will transform our lives and elevate our purpose.

MEDITATION QUESTIONS

1. How do you know if you have been chosen?

____

____

____

____

2. How does God qualify those that have been chosen?

____

____

____

____

3. What has God called you to do?

____

____

____

____

PRAYER FOCUS

Pray that God will remind us of the anointing,
gifting, and calling that he has given us.

Pray that God will remove doubt and fear from our lives.

Pray that God will prepare us for our next level.

NOTES

____

____

____

____

____

____

____

____

____

____

DAY TWELVE

Ephesians 6:10-18

PROTECT YOURSELF

"Wherefore take unto you the whole armor of God, that ye may be able to withstand in the evil day, and having done all, to stand." **(Ephesians 6:13)**

We must never underestimate the devil and the agencies under his control. The devil is not omnipresent, but he is superbly organized. With the assistance of principalities and hosts, he exercises immense influence over the people of the world. Jesus and the Apostles referred to the devil as the ruler or prince or god of this world (John 12:31; 2nd Corinthians 4:4). It is possible to become overwhelmed with fear, whenever we think of the power and authority that the devil and his minions exercise over the world. Let us not be afraid, because we have protection with Jesus on our side. Our God is a kind, gentle Savior who blesses his children. He is also the warrior who fights on our behalf and causes the enemy to flee. We have protection in Jesus Christ and we must use what He has given us to cover and protect ourselves from the attack of the enemy.

The Bible says in Acts 1:8, **"But ye shall receive power, after that the Holy Ghost is come upon you"**. We do not empower ourselves, we receive power from the Holy Ghost, given to us by God. The Holy Ghost enables us access to divine resources. Divine resources that are required in order to protect ourselves from **"the rulers of the darkness of this world"**.

Through Scriptures and our testimonies, Jesus Christ has always proven to supply all of our needs. The Word of God reminds us that we must utilize the armor and weapons that He has given us. We become equipped through Him – it is not by our strength, but by His strength. When we are empowered by the Holy Ghost, we can stand tall in God's authority without fear of failure or defeat.

We are living in very difficult and evil days, and the only way that we can stand victorious, is to protect ourselves with the power of the Holy Ghost that God has given unto us.

We are protected when we put on the armor of God, take up our weapons and stand firm in faith. The Body of Christ is called to resist, wrestle and fight
against the powers of darkness. As a group of unified believers, empowered with the Holy Ghost, we must be ready to advance the Kingdom of God against the forces of evil. It is time to demonstrate great faith in Jesus Christ (Be strong in the Lord…)

- God's word in our minds (belt of truth)
- God's word in our hearts (breastplate of righteousness)
- God's word in our walk (sandals of the gospel of peace)
- God's word in our actions and deeds (shield of faith)
- God's word in our promise of salvation (helmet of salvation)

Lastly, because we are empowered by the Holy Ghost, when we pray in the spirit, we activate a shield of divine protection around us. I believe that when Jesus us how to pray, He included this line in the prayer for an intended purpose: **"And lead us not into temptation, but deliver us from evil…"** (Matthew 6:13). There is a constant need for believers to pray this prayer daily. Oswald Chambers said, **"The devil is a bully, but when we stand in the**
armor of God he cannot harm us; if we tackle him in our own strength, we are soon done for; but if we stand with the strength and courage of God, he cannot gain one inch of way at all." As Believers, we do not need to doubt that we have protection, because Jesus has already promised us that He will be with us always, even unto the end of the world. We just need to keep ourselves covered, through faith, prayer and the Word of God.

MEDITATION QUESTIONS

1. What tools can we use to fight against the enemy?

____

____

____

____

2. How do we protect ourselves from failure, defeat, and destruction?

____

____

____

____

3. In your own words, what is the significance of the Lord's Prayer? And how does it help us in our prayer life?

____

____

____

____

PRAYER FOCUS

Pray that the body of Christ will demonstrate the power of God, by living and walking in the Holy Ghost.

Pray for authority and boldness
(Be Strong in the Lord).

Pray for protection of yourself and your family
(the armor of God).

Pray for victory in every battle.

NOTES

____

____

____

____

____

____

____

____

____

____

DAY THIRTEEN

Daniel 3:19-30

I AM STILL STANDING

"Then Nebuchadnezzar the king was astonished, and rose up in haste, and spake, and said unto his counsellors, did not we cast three men bound into the midst of the fire? They answered and said unto the king, True, O king. He answered and said, Lo, I see four men loose, walking in the midst of the fire, and they have no hurt; and the form of the fourth is like the Son of God." **(Daniel 3:24-26)**

Today's text speaks of Shadrach, Meshach, and Abednego, three men who exemplified the power of great faith while under pressure. The story began with King Nebuchadnezzar, looking for some of the most intelligent, strong, and healthy men to bring into Babylon (Daniel 1:3-4). His goal was to take them from their homes to a place of unfamiliarity in order to train and mold them to be of great help under his leadership.

King Nebuchadnezzar realized that taking these men to Babylon would not separate them from their relationship with God; despite having to learn a new language and experience new literature. While they were in Babylon, King Nebuchadnezzar made a golden statue of himself and decreed that everyone should bow down and worship the statue, whenever they heard the **"music"**. Failure to bow down and worship the golden image would result in being thrown into a fiery furnace. Shadrach, Meshach, and Abednego refused to bow down to the King's statue. When Nebuchadnezzar heard this, he was furious, and ordered that Shadrach, Meshach, and Abednego be brought before him. When they refused to yield to his threats, Nebuchadnezzar ordered that they be thrown into the fire, with the furnace heated seven times hotter. Those that threw Shadrach, Meshach, and Abednego into the fire were killed instantly by the flames. However, the fire had no impact on the three Hebrew men. In fact, King Nebuchadnezzar came to the furnace expecting them to be dead, but instead, saw four men walking around in the fiery furnace unbound and unharmed. Shadrach, Meshach, and Abednego showed a great sense of conviction and commitment to God. They were willing to die holding on to their commitment. God is looking for individuals like those men, who will not compromise their faith while under pressure. God did not deliver these men from being thrown into the fiery furnace, but He delivered them in the fire, revealing his sustaining power. These men were able to stand before the fire, in the fire, and make it through the fire. As a result of God's covering, they did not look like what they had been through. They came out with the testimony of an overcomer (Revelations 12:11). Can God count on us to stand firm in our faith, even when we are in the midst of a fiery situation?

A portion of **"Jesus, I'll Go through with Thee"** written by Mrs. E.E. Williams states, **"…naught from Him my soul can sever while I'm trusting in His word. I the lonely way have taken, rough and toilsome though it be; and although despised, forsaken, Jesus, I'll go thro' with Thee."** These words are a profession of faith that indicates a willingness to go through the tests, storms, and fiery situations of life. It is a song rooted in hope and endurance; an uplifting reminder of our authority to declare, **"I am still standing"**.

MEDITATION QUESTIONS

57

1. Name an experience in your life where you went through a fiery situation but came out standing?

____

____

____

____

2. What is the importance of being rooted and grounded in God?

____

____

____

____

3. How do we survive the storms in our life?

____

____

____

____

PRAYER FOCUS

Pray that God will increase our faith.

❖

Pray for deliverance from fear and doubt.

❖

Pray for boldness to do the Will of God.

NOTES

____

____

____

____

____

____

____

____

____

____

DAY FOURTEEN

Isaiah 9:1-8

THE DAWN IS BREAKING

"The people that walked in darkness have seen a great light: they that dwell in the land of the shadow of death, upon them hath the light shined." **(Isaiah 9:2)**

Darkness is known to be most intense just before the dawn, and despair runs deepest just before there is a breakthrough. Darkness often brings a feeling of helplessness and fear that evil surrounds us. It is unsettling and disturbing for many of us, because it cloaks the intent and the practice of evil. Jesus said to Nicodemus in John 3:19-21 **"And this is the condemnation, that light is come into the world, and men loved darkness rather than light, because their deeds were evil. For every one that doeth evil hateth the light, neither cometh to the light, lest his deeds should be reproved. But he that doeth truth cometh to the light, that his deeds may be made manifest, that they are wrought in God."** The desire of a child of God should always be the light. Light dispels darkness: Where there is light, darkness cannot exist. It is impossible for darkness to overcome light. Light gives direction: Walking in the light helps us to see where we are and where we are going. Light offers discovery: Things are much easier to find when the lights are on. Isaiah chapter six demonstrates the promise of hope for the hopeless and light to those who are walking in darkness. **"The people that walked in darkness have seen a great light: they that dwell in the land of the shadow of death, upon them hath the light shined."** (Isaiah 9:2)

The nation of Israel had been walking in a season of darkness that caused the people to lose hope. God spoke to His people, through the prophet Isaiah amidst their fears and offered hope; that there would be a day when the darkness would be defeated and a new light would dawn for the world. The timing of God could not have come at a more desperate point in history. Israel was suffering immensely under the occupation of Rome and endured one of the worst periods of persecution in their history. Religious freedom was limited, massive deportations took place across the Roman Empire, and they had not heard a prophet from God in nearly 500 years. The prophet Isaiah brought the message to them that **"the dawn is breaking"** symbolizing the Messiah would come.

The people of God will always go through difficulties and adversities. Time on this earth will bring its share of pain and sorrow, but there is always a new day dawning for the Believer. There is always the expectation that God will work whatever happens to us for our good. He promised, **"And we know that all things work together for good to them that love God, to them who are the called according to his purpose"** (Romans 8:28). 1st Corinthians 10:13 states, **"There hath no temptation taken you but such as is common to man: but God is faithful, who will not suffer you to be tempted above that ye are able; but will with the temptation also make a way to escape, that ye may be able to bear it."** Therefore, through Christ, we will not be defeated; and there is always an escape route. We are under God's mighty care because we are His children.

It is said that during the dawn's early light we may not be able to see clearly, as it is not yet fully light. However, we can get excited because we know that in a short while, the dawn will fully break. The outcome of our battles and what we are going through now may not be fully evident, but we can see enough to know that our freedom is won. It is assured; the dawn is breaking.

MEDITATION QUESTIONS

1. It is said, that darkness is most intense just before the dawn and that despair runs deepest just before there is a breakthrough. Do you agree? If so, why?

____

____

____

____

2. As children of God, what give us confidence and strength to endure hardships?

____

____

____

____

3. Do you believe that the **"dawn is breaking"** for you? If so, why?

____

____

____

____

PRAYER FOCUS

Pray for those who are unsaved and backsliders
to draw nigh to God.

Pray that God will give strength to the weak, hope
to the hopeless and faith to the faithless.

Pray for the dawning of a new day in our finances,
health and relationship with God.

Pray that we will not be consumed by the
temptations we face.

NOTES

____

____

____

____

____

____

____

____

____

____

DAY FIFTEEN

2nd Corinthians 5:1-17

PLUG INTO POWER

"Therefore if any man be in Christ, he is a new creature: old things are passed away; behold, all things are become new." **(2nd Corinthians 5:17)**

Our text makes a claim which some people may find hard to believe concerning the theme of a life makeover. This speaks of a total spiritual makeover of a person who is in Christ. This type of change requires that the old must go and something new must take its place. For those of us who have attempted to make any significant change in our lives, we are aware of the difficulty of the process. We have the desire to change, but the power to influence such a change may seem improbable.

Take a moment and reflect on this scenario: An electrician using a cordless drill requires a charged battery to work efficiently. Therefore, a drill with a dead battery is ineffective, because the battery is its' power source. The drill has to be plugged into its' power source in order to be useful. The stronger the power source, the better the drill works. Our power source as a child of God is the Holy Ghost. Without the Spirit of Christ, we are unable to successfully function as a Christian. Without plugging into Christ, we will find ourselves lacking the spiritual charge that is necessary to be transformed from that which is broken to that which is whole.

The power to change must initiate the power to remove the old and bring in the new. This becomes even more challenging in relation to personal change. The old has become engrained in us and it is quite difficult, if not impossible to undo the past. In essence, we have become a product of everything we have done and everything that has been done to us. Although we all desire to experience a change in our lives, the old doesn't want to go and the new always seems to be just beyond our reach. We need something beyond our human capabilities to initiate real change in our lives. To access the power to change, we must get ourselves plugged into the power source. This power source is the power of Christ; the resurrection power that raised Christ from the dead. It is the only power that is able to bring about a real and lasting change.

Jesus describes the divine connection between Him and His followers, to that of a vine and branches (John 15:5). The vine gives us life, and while connected to Jesus, we have life and bear fruit. Adam's sin unplugged us from God, our life giving source, but He came to reconnect us. When we have strayed from God, repentance is the cord that plugs us back in. Prayer provides the current that flows through the cord; and the Holy Ghost is the power that enables us. We can be confident that no matter what we experience, we have access to everything that we need to overcome. Many are fearful of the future and are desperately clinging to the past. There is an uncertainty in our spirit as to whether or not we will survive the times we are in. I encourage you to cancel the noise and commotion, turn away from the confusion and chaos and look to Jesus who is the answer. We know where the power lies, all we have to do is get plugged in and let God flow through us.

MEDITATION QUESTIONS

1. Our power source is the Holy Ghost. How do we become connected?

2. Is the Holy Ghost indicative of immediate change?

3. What is the importance of maintaining our connection?

PRAYER FOCUS

Pray for consistent unity in the spirit.

Pray for a spiritual transformation in the lives of believers.

Pray that God will remove anything that hinders our connection to Him.

Pray for a spiritual recharge.

NOTES

DAY SIXTEEN

Acts 2:37-47

CONNECTED TO GROWTH

"And all that believed were together, and had all things common."
(Acts 2:44)

Redwood trees in California are the largest living things on earth and the tallest trees in the world. Some of them are 100 meters high and more than 2,500 years old. You would think that trees this large would have a tremendous root system, but this is not the case. Redwoods trees have a shallow root system; and their roots are intertwined. They are interlocked and remain unshakeable through mighty storms and winds. With an interlocking root system, they support and sustain each other. Just as the Redwood tree needs one another to survive, so do we as children of God.

We are able to grow spiritually mature in a God-ordained environment called the church. We stand strong because we belong to a community of faith. God has given us His Church, which is the body of Christ on earth. When one is baptized into Christ, one is baptized into the body of Christ. Through Christ we are bound together in a community of faith. Since we belong to Christ, we belong to each other. Everybody that God calls is given an assignment. Growth is not an option for the children of God, it is a requirement. It is more than just an expectation on the church's part; it is a commandment from God.

From Genesis to Revelation – the Bible paints a picture of community, from the Garden of Eden to the Jerusalem City at the end. We are created for relationship. The church is a God-designed support system. As such, it is intended to meet some crucial needs in our lives. Growth can only take place in a flourishing environment; and this environment is the church. In other words, we cannot grow without the church. We can never really grow in maturity, if we are away from the constant presence of God's people. Hebrews 10:25, **"Not forsaking the assembling of ourselves together, as the manner of some is; but exhorting one another: and so much the more…"** This is why it is very important that we remain faithful in our attendance to worship with the people of God. Coming together keeps us connected to growth. Even if we are going through a difficult time, struggling with some problem or sin, the last place we want to be is away from God's people. The church is one of the mechanisms God uses to bring grace and strength into our lives.

Acts 2:44 says, **"…All that believed were together…"** The picture being painted here is not of a strong Christian, but rather of a strong Church. The believers were under persecution, but were able to overcome, because they were together. They obtained individual strength from the corporate strength of the Church. We are strong today, because we are connected in the body of Christ. We are able to overcome discouragement, doubts, temptations and trials, because we belong to a church. God has given us each other. God expects us to be there for each other. I encourage each of us to make the Church a priority in our lives and to stay connected.

Give priority to the church. In his book The Connecting Church, Author Randy Frazee writes: **"The writings of Scripture lead one to conclude that God intends the church, not to be one more bolt on the wheel of activity in our lives, but the very hub at the center of one's life…"** We are not called to do this Christian journey alone. God has given us this family, **"members of God's household"** (Ephesians 2:19). It is absolutely essential that we stay close to the church for strength and guidance. Therefore, let's make this community of faith a priority in our lives. Be devoted to it, the same way the believers in the book of Acts were.

MEDITATION QUESTIONS

1. Why do we need to grow as Christians?

____

____

____

____

____

2. Acts 2:44 says, **"...and all that believed were together..."** Why is this statement important for us as a Church?

____

____

____

____

____

3. What factors affect our ability to make the Church a priority?

____

____

____

____

PRAYER FOCUS

Pray for growth through the forgiveness of sins.

❖

Pray that we will overcome disappointments,
discouragements and failures.

❖

Pray for strength to continue progressing in faith and ministry.

❖

Pray for a deeper connection to Christ.

NOTES

DAY SEVENTEEN

Joel 2:25-32

RESTORING THE YEARS

"And I will restore to you the years that the locust hath eaten, the cankerworm, and the caterpillar, and the palmerworm, my great army which I sent among you." (**Joel 2:25**)

The Merriam-Webster dictionary defines restoration as the bringing back to a former position or condition. In other words, restoration is the reinstatement or return of someone or something back to a former condition, place, or position. In order to obtain complete restoration, we must position ourselves to receive it. The first step is to acknowledge the need for restoration, then we humbly go to God in repentance and commune with Him through prayer.

Joel is one of the Minor Prophets of the Bible. The central themes in this prophetic book of Joel are judgement and God's grace. Joel prophesied at a time of great devastation in the land of Judah. The Bible tells us that a vast plague of locus had stripped the land of Judah of all its vegetation, destroyed the pasture of the sheep and cattle, and stripped the fig tree completely bare (Joel 1:4-7). Within a short space of time, the entire land of Judah was stripped of everything. The plague of locus that Joel wrote about was greater than what anyone had ever seen, all of the crops were lost and the seed crop for the next season had all been destroyed. A famine and drought had seized the entire land; both humans and animals were dying. It was so profound and disastrous, that Joel saw only one explanation for this calamity, God's judgement (Joel 2:1-2).

We all have an appointment with destiny, and we should not be complacent and assume that we are exempt from God's judgement. The prophecy of Joel indicates that four separate and distinct attacks of the locus destroyed all of the vegetation. God had already told Israel through Solomon, **"If I shut up heaven that there be no rain, or if I command the locusts to devour the land, or if I send pestilence among my people; If my people, which are called by my name, shall humble themselves, and pray, and seek my**

face, and turn from their wicked ways; then will I hear from heaven, and will forgive their sin, and will heal their land" (2nd Chronicles 7:13-14). Now the Lord is telling His people that He is going to give back that which the locus has destroyed. Sometimes the plan of the enemy becomes overwhelming and causes us to feel defeated. When it looks like everything is in ruin, be assured, it is not over until God says it is over. God is going to restore unto us, the years that the locus has destroyed. Today's text comes as a reminder that God can and will restore unto us everything that the devil has taken from us. This includes, but is not limited to, the restoration of our health, finances, marriages, and spiritual relationship with Him.

The Bible says in Joel 2:28 that, **"It shall come to pass afterward, that I will pour out my spirit upon all flesh; and your sons and your daughters shall prophesy, your old men shall dream dreams, your young men shall see visions"**. After God restores unto us the years that were stolen from us, His Word says, that He is going to pour out His Spirit. We will walk in the overflow of a fresh anointing and a higher level of spiritual awareness. We serve a God of restoration; and our latter days will be greater than our past.

MEDITATION QUESTIONS

73

1. What does restoration mean to you?

____

____

____

____

2. What areas of your life are you seeking God to restore?

____

____

____

____

3. How can we have complete restoration in God?

____

____

____

____

PRAYER FOCUS

Pray that God will grant complete restoration
to those who have suffered great loss.

Pray for a spirit of obedience and patience as we wait on God
to pour out a fresh overflow of His Spirit.

NOTES

____

____

____

____

____

____

____

____

____

____

DAY EIGHTEEN

John 5:1-16

WAITING ON GOD

"Jesus saith unto him, Rise, take up thy bed, and walk. And immediately the man was made whole, and took up his bed, and walked: and on the same day was the Sabbath." (**John 5:8-9**)

Our text takes us to Jerusalem to a pool that is named **"Bethesda"** which is translated, **"House of Mercy"**. Many people could be found in this place of mercy, which had not yet received mercy and were sick, blind, and lame. I believe many of God's people can testify that at one time or another, they were living in a situation similar to individuals sitting at the pool of mercy waiting for help.

As believers of Christ, we are called to be kings and priests, yet many of us are sitting by our inheritance, gasping for life, and unable to take the necessary steps towards deliverance. We can be in a place of mercy, yet feel bound by our environment and circumstances. The Bible tells us that those of us who have been set free by Jesus are free indeed, yet many of us are still living blind, lame and paralyzed lives. We are lame in the sense that we have been stuck in one place for a long time, and paralyzed from doing anything about our condition.

Verse 3 of our text states, **"…in these lay a great multitude of sick people, blind, lame, paralyzed, waiting for the moving of the water."** This is the condition that many of God's people are in today, waiting a change in their circumstances. Many of us have been going to Church, waiting, and as a result of Covid-19, we are at home, waiting.

The reflective question we must ask ourselves is, why are we waiting on God to solve problems He solved over 2,000 years ago?

God already proclaimed freedom for the prisoners, recovery of sight for the blind and freedom for the oppressed (Luke 4:18). The mission of Christ on earth was to save us, deliver us, and empower us to dominate our environment and earthly situations. He accomplished this on the cross; and sent the Holy Ghost to empower us. We no longer need to sit by the pool of despair. The potential we require to overcome is within us.

In verse 6 of the lesson, Jesus asked the man **"…wilt thou be made whole?"**, the Amplified Bible **"…do you want to get well?"** I believe that this is a pertinent question for us today. Notice that Jesus did not address the whole crowd assembled by the pool, nor did He heal the entire group. It was personal visitation for this man and we too can receive our own personal visitation. The sick man answered him, **"Sir, I have no man, when the water is troubled, to put me into the pool: but while I am coming, another steppeth down before me"** (John 5:7). This man was waiting for someone to help him, to no avail. Jesus said to him, **"Rise, take up your bed and walk."** and immediately the man was made whole. The response of Jesus was anticlimactic; He did not pray for him, help to get him into the water or spoke in tongues. Jesus spoke to the potential in the man, and the ability he did not know he possessed.

What excuses do you give yourself for your lack of progress with God or with life? Are you waiting on your family, your boss or your Pastor? It is time to lay aside the weight that so easily besets us (Hebrews 12:1), and press forward towards our change.

MEDITATION QUESTIONS

1. What does it mean to wait on God?

____

____

____

____

____

2. The man at the pool remained in a stagnant position for 38 years. Do you think he had valid reasons for being in this condition for so long?

____

____

____

____

____

3. Do you believe that many people already have the answer they are waiting for? If so, how can they identify the answer?

____

____

____

____

____

PRAYER FOCUS

Prayer for those who are in a season of waiting.

Pray that our soul will be strengthened and our faith fortified
while we wait on God.

Pray for patience and understanding to answered prayers,
whether delayed or denied.

Pray for a renewed level of faith in God's timing.

NOTES

DAY NINETEEN

Mark 9:1-13

GLORY ON THE OTHER SIDE

"And after six days Jesus taketh with him Peter, and James, and John, and leadeth them up into a high mountain apart by themselves: and He was transfigured before them. And His raiment became shining, exceeding white as snow; so as no fuller on earth can white them." **(Mark 9:2-3)**

As believers and followers of Christ, we will face suffering. 2nd Timothy 2:12 says, **"If we suffer, we shall also reign with Him"**. In this Scripture, Paul reminds us that the suffering we experience is not the end of our story but a source of our testimony. On the other side of our suffering is God's Glory. Prior to His death, Jesus appeared to Peter, James, and John. After six days, He took them up to a high mountain where He was transfigured before their eyes. This transformation revealed the Glory of God to the disciples. The Bible tells us that **"His raiment became shining, exceeding white as snow; so as no fuller on earth can white them"**. The disciples were encouraged, knowing that on other side of suffering, persecution, and death was a manifestation of His Glory.

Some of us have endured many hardships in our lives, but we survived. We are still in our right minds and we still have a praise. What the enemy designed for our demise, God will turn around for our good. I believe that God will open the windows of Heaven in our lives. There will be a supernatural transformation that will change us forever. God did not allow us to go through all that we have gone through, only to come out as a survivor. Our status can and will be changed from a survivor to an overcomer. We are overcomers by the blood of the lamb, and by the word of our testimony (Revelation 12:11).

God has a plan for a glorious Church without spots or wrinkles. God's plan has not been altered because of the condition of the church or the world. God will glorify His Church and protect us from the plan of the enemy. In

Jerusalem, the old temple was full of splendor and glory, and its' outward beauty was very attractive. After the return from Babylon, the new temple was not as outwardly attractive. Many failed to realize that the temple was glorious, but not based on its' outward appearance. In the Old Testament God had a temple for His people; while in the New Testament God has a people for His temple. 1ˢᵗ Corinthians 3:16 **"Know ye not that ye are the temple of God, and that the Spirit of God dwelleth in you?"** The next time you look at yourself in the mirror, remind yourself that you are not merely looking at an outward beautiful/handsome form, but you are looking at the temple of Yahweh! In Haggai 2:9, the prophet states **"The glory of this latter house shall be greater than of the former"**. Therefore, no matter what we go through, we are His temple, and there will be glory after this!

MEDITATION QUESTIONS

1. Reflect on a time when you endured suffering. How did you overcome?

____

____

____

____

2. How do you explain, 1ˢᵗ Corinthians 3:16, "**...ye are the temple of God...?**"

____

____

____

____

3. What is the significance of God's Glory being revealed in our lives?

____

____

____

____

PRAYER FOCUS

Pray that God will heal every physical illness,
pain, and hereditary disease.

Pray that God will give us confidence in what
He has revealed unto us.

Pray that God will help us to understand the importance of
our bodies as **"God's temple"**.

NOTES

DAY TWENTY

Hebrews 10:19-25

PRESSING ON

"Let us hold fast the profession of our faith without wavering; (for he is faithful that promised..." **(Hebrews 10:23)**

"Wherefore seeing we also are compassed about with so great a cloud of witnesses, let us lay aside every weight, and the sin which doth so easily beset us, and let us run with patience the race that is set before us." **(Hebrews 12:1)**

This amazing race of our Christian journey can be very strenuous at times. In order to endure, we must be strong, courageous, and determined in our pursuit. God has called us to Himself for a purpose. He wants us to know Him and make Him known. Everything else that we think our life is about is minuscule in comparison to our life in Christ Jesus. Christ wants us to press on, through the failures and adversities that surround us. It is time for us to take hold of the very thing for which He died, eternal life. Christ wants us to press on in our faith, never arriving but always moving forward. He wants us to press on in our calling to make Christ known in a sick and sinful world. Heroes of the faith are not perfect people, but they are determined, **"...but this one thing I do, forgetting those things which are behind, and reaching forth unto those things which are before."** (Philippians 3:13)

Our text in Hebrews 10 takes us to a time when Israel, Gods people were going through a very difficult period. Some were tempted to detach themselves from their Christian fellowship in order to avoid arrest, reproach, and suffering. Moreover, some were in danger of turning their backs on Christianity and reverting to Judaism.

They had suffered persecution for their faith and they endured numerous obstacles for the Gospel. Life was so overwhelming that they were unsure if they would overcome. I am sure many of us can identify and relate to a time when we have endured hardships similar to that of the Children of Israel.

How do you continue pressing forward when it seems that life is against you, with no hope in sight? What do we say to someone who is tired and just wants to give up? How do you encourage them to endure? In Hebrews 10:19 we are shown the importance of pressing on. He reminds us of our hope so we can carry on – **"Let us hold fast the profession of our faith without wavering; (for he is faithful that promised…"**

As children of God, how we finish our Christian journey matters more than how we have begun. At some point, we will arrive at a place where we feel as if everything in our life is falling apart. In spite of our battles, we must learn how to endure the hardships of this world. When you are in the midst of hardship, it is difficult to see your breakthrough, but we must remind ourselves that God is in control.

In Hebrews 10:35-36, it reads **"Cast not away therefore your confidence, which hath great recompense of reward. For ye have need of patience, that, after ye have done the will of God, ye might receive the promise"**. It is inevitable that we will face challenges to our faith. Some of us have been targets of persecution, yet we've maintained our commitment to Jesus Christ. In spite of the times we are in and the challenges we face, I encourage you to maintain your confidence in Christ and keep pressing on.

MEDITATION QUESTIONS

85

1. Proskarteresis which is Greek for perseverance means endurance and continuance. What is the value of perseverance to a child of God?`

___

2. What does **"forgetting things behind…"** mean to you?

___

3. How do we continue pressing on when life seems to be against us?

___

PRAYER FOCUS

Prayer for patience, perseverance and endurance.

Pray for strength in times of persecution and opposition.

Pray for the young people and the future of the church, that
they will persevere against all odds.

NOTES

____

____

____

____

____

____

____

____

____

____

DAY TWENTY-ONE

Philippians 3:1-14

DETERMINED TO WIN

Fight the good fight of faith, lay hold on eternal life, whereunto thou art also called, and hast professed a good profession before many witnesses." **(1ˢᵗ Timothy 6:12)**

Paul wrote to Timothy and told him in 1ˢᵗ Timothy 6:12 **"Fight the good fight of faith, lay hold on eternal life …"** he then told him in 2ⁿᵈ Timothy 4:7-8 **"I have fought a good fight, I have finished my course, I have kept the faith: Henceforth there is laid up for me a crown of righteousness."** At the end of his life, Paul told Timothy that the connection between a "kept" faith is going to be a **"fought for"** faith. We must have a determined sprit in order to obtain the prize. We have to press on and fight at every turn in our lives, in both private and public. We must have a mindset that refuses to be defeated despite huge setbacks and obstacles.

This is the same Paul who wrote to the Church at Philippi and said in Philippians 3:13-14 **"Brethren, I count not myself to have apprehended: but this one thing I do, forgetting those things which are behind, and reaching forth unto those things which are before, I press toward the mark for the prize of the high calling of God in Christ Jesus."** This is the Spirit of faith that Paul fought for and that the church today will have to fight for. Until truth takes hold of our mind and heart, it will never become real or fruitful. Many of us are guilty of living on the perimeters of faith and which is why we've failed to receive total transformation. Over the course of time, the steady fight of faith has caused men and women to mature. Even in the darkest and most dangerous hours of our life, we must continue forward.

Paul's advice for us in our day is that we should stand firm and hold true to the course that has been plotted out for us.

We must endure the afflictions that come with the course. When we read through 2ⁿᵈ Timothy 4, we find Paul dealing with much afflictions and troubles, such as being whipped, beaten and stoned. Demos forsake him and Alexander committed much evil towards him.

God also placed support along the way to assist such as Aquila, Priscilla, Luke, Crescens, and Erastus. Paul knew that if he would fight for the faith every day, there will come a time that the faith he fought for will be the faith that will keep him.

Another biblical example refers to the woman with the issue of blood in Luke 8:43 who was determined to receive healing. In Mark 5, Jairus' daughter died, but he remained determined. As we face our future, let us be willing to be uncomfortable, misunderstood, criticized or persecuted as we press forward.

Regardless of what is ahead of us, we must have the determination to win. In spite of our setbacks, we must continue in worship and prayer through the challenges we face. I believe that God is preparing us to endure, so that in the end, we will be able to say **"I win"**.

MEDITATION QUESTIONS

1. How would you describe a person that has the determination to win?

____

____

____

____

____

2. In spite of all that Paul went through, he had people in his life to help him. What can we do to ensure that we have a strong support system?

____

____

____

____

3. How do you get reenergized after you have suffered a setback?

____

____

____

____

PRAYER FOCUS

Pray for courage, restoration and determination.

Pray, we will persevere to finish our Christian race.

Pray for self-examination, honesty and spiritual growth in the lives of God's people.

Pray for victory over sin.

NOTES

____

____

____

____

____

____

____

____

____

____

BIBLIOGRAPHY

Anderson, AnnMarie. "How to Trust God's Timing." Busy Blessed Women, 31 Dec. 2020, busyblessedwomen.com/how-to-trust-godstiming/.

"Chosen." Merriam-Webster, Merriam-Webster, www.merriam-webster.com/dictionary/chosen.

Daniel Olukoya, "The Enemy Has Done This" 2003. Oswald Chambers:https://www.azquotes.com/author/2691 -Oswald_Chambers.

Holy Bible: Authorized King James Version. Grand Rapids, MI: Zondervan, 2000.

https://www.biblegateway.com/resources/asbury-bible-commentary

"Loosed." Merriam-Webster, Merriam-Webster, 2011, www.merriam-webster.com/dictionary/loosed.

"Losing Your Way." Sermon Central, 24 Sept. 2007, www.sermoncentral.com/sermons/losing-your-way-tom-fuller -sermon-on-bible-influence-112 106.

Michael A. Turner [Pulpit Resource, Logos Productions Inc., 2008]

"Restoration." Merriam-Webster.com. Merriam-Webster, 2011, www.merriam-webster.com/dictionary/restoration.

Williams, Mrs. E. E. "Jesus, I'll Go through with Thee." Hymnary.org

www.ingramcontent.com/pod-product-compliance
Lightning Source LLC
Chambersburg PA
CBHW061430050726
47593CB00006B/2292